NEVER GOING TO BE A HERO

A HEROES COLLECTION SHORT STORY

ALEXANDRIA BLAELOCK

BlueMere Books
MELBOURNE, AUSTRALIA

For permission requests, please contact enquiries@bluemerebooks.com.

Ordering Information:
Discounts are available on quantity purchases. For details, contact orders@bluemerebooks.com.

Never Going to be a Hero/Alexandria Blaelock
paperback ISBN: 978-1-922744-25-8
digital ISBN: 978-1-922744-26-5

NEVER GOING TO BE A HERO

If Veronica was on a planet, she'd be in one of those odd job kiosks at the bottom of the train station or parking structure. The kind of kiosk you can drop off your dry cleaning, appliances to be fixed, keys to be cut in the morning and pick them up in the evening.

The kind of kiosk that's so filthy with decades of train and parking dust and grime you wonder whether you'll need a tetanus shot to just walk past it.

And smells like generations of men have relieved themselves on the side of it.

That's almost obscured by cardboard sheets of key rings, carabiners and penknives you don't want to touch with a barge pole, that don't seem to sell, and have been there so long they've curled inward at the edges.

That never seems to have any business, yet never shuts down, and makes you wonder if it just exists to launder drug money.

But Veronica, also known as Vee, lives on Mephisto station, and they don't have basements.

At one end of the scale, you can get a large luxury apartment in the core, with plant supplemented oxygen, simulated sunlight, barely recycled water and oxygen, and reliable gravity.

Well, you can, if you can afford it...

Or if, like Vee, you want something cheap, you'll find it on the edge where the gravity is less than reliable, oxygen not as well-scrubbed, and if there's a meteor strike or someone crash-lands you might lose your home.

Technically, units on the edge are zoned for industrial and commercial purposes only, with communal kitchens and washrooms set at intervals around the rim. But that's where Vee, and the poorest of the poor live.

Not because she's destitute, but because she doesn't want to attract attention.

She's going straight now.

And she feels like she owes it to humanity to make amends.

Vee's unit, like all the others, was an empty, more or less rectangular room measuring twenty-four square metres, with a safety glass frontage so people can see what you're selling.

The light from the main corridors forms a useful supplement to the three strip lights inside.

The lights are controlled by one light switch, and the empty unit also contained two power sockets, one air outlet and one communications hub access point.

She installed a counter at the front, shelves and workbenches in the middle, and a tiny area behind the last shelving unit to sleep in.

And added one air freshener approximating the smell of lavender, rosemary and fresh air to counteract the smell of boiled cabbage coming from the air outlet.

And may have illegally jury-rigged the power outlets.

Vee buys, sells and repairs small electronics, so the shelves are crammed with bits and pieces of housing, wires, transistors, capacitors, diodes, bits of circuit board, switches, connectors and other useful things.

The inners throw out a lot of stuff when it stops working, so their day workers (who live in the outer), fish it out of the bins and sell it to Vee to supplement their meagre wages. At least, that's what they do when they don't get caught.

Vee breaks them into components and uses them to repair the toasters and rice cookers the outers rely on and can't afford to replace.

When the outers do get caught, the inners generally demand the goods back so they can throw them out properly. Then they sack the outers (as they are easily replaceable), and demand penalties that generally amount to several days' wages.

Which is why Vee also scours the garbage dumps for items that might be useful one day.

Sometimes the inner's fancy food doesn't make it to the bin either. Somehow it gets to the black market too.

And because you never know when you might need a favour, it's not uncommon that Vee might be offered a wafer-thin slice of cake on someone's birthday.

She also practises a bit of field dentistry and medicine, when you've been injured and don't want anyone asking too many questions.

Or when you're skint and can't afford a proper doctor, she only charges for the goods and not her time.

That's why she's very popular with the outers, and they'll often call in for a chat. And because she chats, she always knows a fella who can get you what you need.

It was a kind of life that suited Vee well. She was more or less at ease. With people who were more or less friends.

It'd been a few years, and she was just starting to let her guard down...

She was sharing a glass of rotgut with Tim as she picked bits of industrial drill from his leg when he said, "I've heard a rumour Black Eyed Benny's on the station."

She helped herself to another shot, and pored one for him, "isn't there a warrant out for his arrest?"

"He came in via the smuggler's route," meaning someone had shipped him in as cargo, "word is, he's looking for someone."

"Any idea who?" she asked, taking advantage of his out-breath to pull a shard from his leg.

He gasped and knocked his drink back.

"Isn't that more or less your department?"

She grunted, and smoothed her bloodstained hands down his leg, looking for lumps that might indicate other fragments that needed removing.

Tim grunted and poured another round, drinking his almost immediately.

"Haven't heard anything, but if he's here, Ping can't be far behind."

"She's that psycho bitch from the Jade Dragon triad?"

Vee grunted in agreement as she pulled a threaded needle from her kit.

Tim gritted his teeth while she and quickly and neatly stitched the wounds up, and added a layer of non-stick dressing to each wound.

"You're not going to listen if I tell you to take a day off, are you?"

He grinned, "I got a wife and kids to support."

She drank her drink, and grinned as she poured two more, "thought you'd say that. Try to go easy on that leg, and take one of these pills when the pain gets bad, but be warned, it'll knock you out."

She sighed as she handed him two green pills.

There was no point Tim asking for protective equipment when there were others who'd work without it.

And there was no point going to the company doctor because if he did, he'd be out of a job.

"If you can't get a leather apron, wear your thickest pants dunderhead," she punched his shoulder, "they're better than nothing."

He sighed too, and held his drink up to salute her, "thanks Vee."

She clinked it with hers, "your good health."

He stood to leave, "here, take the bottle," she said.

"But your fee—"

"I think you need it more than me, you take it and bring me another some other time."

He nodded and turned away. She walked him out and watched him hobble away.

Then turned in the other direction and went for a bowl of spicy noodles, with whatever they were passing off as meat that day.

There was no point locking the door, if anyone wanted to get in, they would.

But, in general, people were more often asking for favours of her, so it was in their best interests to make sure she and her stuff were all okay.

Also, the good stuff was stored somewhere else, and anyone with a lick of sense would figure that out.

The main thing was to collect data about Ben and Ping, because despite what she'd said to Tim, she knew Ben was looking for her.

He was an old boyfriend who wouldn't take no for an answer, followed by Ping who wanted to be his new girlfriend.

Lucky she'd been a Jade Dragon liaison at the time and knew how to take care of herself.

Not to mention friendly with the Jade Dragon Mountain Master, and having bought out her contract was leaving the organisation on friendly terms.

It was a shame she wasn't permitted to kill Ben as a condition of her unencumbered release.

Though she'd shot him three times to slow him down.

And slipped him twice before, but dammit, she was sick of running.

She liked Mephisto station, there were good people here.

And quite aside from that, she liked the retro-architecture.

She'd made a mistake thinking Ping would keep him out of her hair.

Ping, for her poor deluded part, wanted him to love her, to want to be with her.

She wasn't keen to keep him banged up, and for that matter, his job in the Jade Dragon didn't really allow for that.

Vee'd always had a problem asking others for help, and Ping wasn't much good at doing favours anyway.

As she ate her noodles, people stopped to chat.

Bought her a drink, dropped off bits and pieces they thought might be useful.

She twisted some wires into a small animal, maybe a dog, though neither she nor the child she made it for had ever seen one.

But more importantly, they passed on information.

It seemed Ben was on-station and waving her picture about.

She'd made some small cosmetic changes through a friend of a friend of a Jade Dragon surgeon, so his photo and description wouldn't be much use.

Nor any of the names he was asking for.

If Ping had arrived, she was keeping a low profile.

Potentially, Vee still had some time to make plans.

She forced herself to walk as slowly as if it was an ordinary day and she had all the time in the world.

As if she wasn't worried about anything.

And as she walked, she paused here and there to talk. Laying her hands on people, in celebration, in commiseration, and not that they knew it, but in blessing.

Worrying about what might happen to them and station if she couldn't keep it safe.

When she got back to her room, it seemed nothing had been disturbed.

Only the lingering scent of sandalwood betrayed the fact that someone more fastidious than the usual spacer had been in her shop.

She glanced at the atmosphere monitor she'd altered to detect common poisons and it was clear.

Closing her eyes, and focusing on her other senses, she couldn't hear breathing, the room was still, and remained at one standard unit of gravity.

Aside from the sandalwood, there were no other scents.

She opened her eyes, and looking with more intention, saw the path Sandalwood had taken through the shop where they'd picked up items and set them down inexactly.

The displaced objects suggested a weird kind of tenderness, that only someone familiar with her deep past would have known about. A badly made cup. A charm bracelet. A puzzle box.

If Sandalwood was Ben, it might be enough to trigger his suspicion.

The perfume of sandalwood was stronger as she proceeded through the room to her tiny sleeping space, and there on the bed, was a folded green robe topped with a sword, and a green object about the size of her fist.

At first, she thought it was a plastic ball of something, but when she picked it up, she realised it was carved stone.

Jade.

Smooth on the bottom, but the dragon ridges so sharp on the top she'd cut herself before she realised.

A jade dragon.

She put her hand to her lips and sucked the edge of it.

The green robe signified Justice, the balance between order and chaos.

The jade dragon statue represented the authority to dispense Justice; protecting the deserving and punishing those who go against the Order of the Jade Dragon.

Lastly, the sword, said to have been passed down to the chosen one for hundreds of generations, representing the threat, and in some cases, the action of Justice.

The Mountain Master had summoned her to join the triad tribunal.

Theoretically, she could refuse...

But she wouldn't be putting any odds on herself to survive, because whoever the envoy was, they'd be watching.

Not Ben of course, it would be someone she didn't know.

On the other hand, taking the green robe offered a promotion of a sort. A role outside the triad, dispensing justice when required.

Not exactly in, not exactly out.

Her word as law.

Her only real option was to wait for the summons.

She didn't have to wait long.

A couple of days later, one of the station urchins who lived in the walls brought a sandalwood scented envelope. The card within told her when and where to go, and nothing else.

In triad Justice, you didn't know who your judge was, or what the charges were before you got the summons.

On the designated evening she set off with the robe, statue and sword stuffed into a backpack, and a couple of daggers in her boots, and got as close as she could without being detected.

Then she donned the robe, pulling the hood forward to hide her face.

She took a deep breath, letting the vestigial sandalwood scent sit in her lungs for a moment, before breathing out her fear and continuing her journey.

She swept into the warehouse, sword in her left hand, statue in the right.

As she ascended the makeshift podium, the excited voices of the witnesses rose.

As she sat in the large chair in the centre of the podium, placing the dragon on the arm of the chair and holding the sword in both hands in her lap, the voices died away.

She was grateful the sandalwood incense masked the smell of unwashed people.

Three people stepped out from the crowd.

A tall man she hadn't seen before walked toward her, bowed, and outlined the charges.

She assumed he was the Master's envoy.

Essentially, the first guy was encroaching on the territory of the second guy. The first guy was invited to address her, and then the second.

Generally, territory was sacrosanct, though if you didn't fully exploit the rights of the territory, it was open to others who would do so.

Vee raised the sheathed sword to pointed towards the second guy, who smiled and bowed. The first guy took a step forward and started arguing with her.

She pulled the sword a couple of inches from its scabbard, and he fell silent.

"The Justice has spoken," the envoy said, repeating the judgement for all to hear, to record it for the Master, and the central records.

The second case involved the theft of stolen goods. She didn't listen to the arguments they made; chances are they were both liars.

Instead, she watched the body language as they spoke. One seemed more open, and the other closed, so she found in favour of the open.

The third case involved people smuggling. The goods had not arrived in a saleable condition. Too many had died in transit, and the cost of saving those who had arrived was too much.

Vee didn't even bother listening to the arguments, just tapped the tip of the sheathed sword on the floor, and beckoned the envoy to approach.

He knelt before her.

"Confiscate the goods to my control," she said.

He looked up under her hood, searching what he could see of her face, and after a pause, nodded.

Declaring the result, and the end of the day's proceedings.

Vee waited for a moment, then picked up the statue in her right hand, and walked out, once again carrying the sword in her left.

This was where it would get tricky; in the robe, with the sword, she was obvious, and needed to get far enough away to disrobe and stuff the gear into the backpack without anyone noticing her.

And then get back to the shop so she could hide it without anyone noticing anything suspicious.

Luck, and her deep familiarity with the station was on her side.

She sat at her workstation, surrounded by bits and bobs of wires, and heaved a sigh of relief.

Of course, if she had to regularly dispense Justice, she wouldn't be able to keep her Jade Dragon connection a secret.

Though she wasn't entirely sure she'd managed this time.

But for the moment, she'd take a drink and let her heart rate settle.

She heard the door open, and then she heard a snick as the bolt shot home.

She tensed, ready to reach for the daggers still in her boots.

And then she caught a scent she'd almost forgotten; bergamot, patchouli and musk.

Ben.

On top of everything else.

How tiresome.

"I found you," he said in a sing-song voice, and she couldn't help but roll her eyes.

How could he be the same when she had changed so much?

"What do you want?"

He laughed, "I want you of course!"

"Well, I don't want you. How many times do I have to tell you?"

Not for the first time she thought wistfully of applying one, or both, of the daggers in her boots to assorted soft tissues in his body.

All she needed now, was Ping to turn up.

And almost as soon as she'd formed the thought, the safety glass door shattered, and Ping stepped through the pieces.

As if the day couldn't get any worse.

Ping launched into a verbal offensive, mainly directed at Ben.

Vee didn't bother listening, she'd heard it twice before, she focused on quickly and silently withdrawing, hopefully before either of them realised what she was up to.

As she reached the counter, she noticed the envoy leaning on a wall a couple of shops down, paring his fingernails with a knife.

He gave her no indication he'd seen her, but the swift, sure movements of the knife gave her an idea.

As a Justice of the triad, her word was law; she could put an official end to this.

She wondered if she dared.

Turning around, she saw Ping had bailed Ben up against a shelving unit. Sensible of him not to have harmed her, given she was a blood relative of the Master, one who had a shot at becoming the Master herself at some point.

They clearly had an easy familiarity with each other's bodies.

"I just don't understand what you see in her," Ping said, looking up at him with tears glistening between her eyelashes.

Vee rolled her eyes.

"Why is it her, and not me?" Ping continued.

Vee made retching noises, and they turned to look at her as if they'd forgotten her.

"Really?" she said, "really?"

She leant on the counter and pointed at Ping.

"You are a criminal mastermind. You basically run half the galaxy, and all you really care about what he does and where he goes?"

She turned to point at Ben, "despite everything, you almost always end going back to Ping. Why do you have to annoy me and everyone in the galaxy with this nonsense?"

Ping glared at her, "how dare you interfere in Jade Dragon business, you should leave before I get annoyed and kill you."

"You can't kill her," Ben said, "I'll kill you before you get to her."

"I'd rather be dead than listen to this crap for a minute longer," Vee said, and put the Jade Dragon and sword on the counter.

Ben gasped, and Ping stepped away from him.

"Right," said Vee, "Ben, give me your best shot."

Ben spluttered, but paused too long.

"Ping?"

Likewise, Ping was caught out.

"Well then, this is my Justice." She walked across to Ben, and pushed him to the ground.

"Ben, you will be contracted to Ping for one Earth standard year. You may not leave her side unless she tells you to.

"Ping, when the year is up, you must let him go. Whether he chooses to stay with you or not is up to him.

"Further, Justices must remain independent, and apart, so neither of you may approach me again.

"Ping, take this useless piece of shit, and get the hell off my station."

Ping laughed, "you have no one to record your judgement, so it's not binding."

"On the contrary," the envoy's voice said from behind Vee, "the Justice has spoken, and her word is the law."

"Come on Ping," Ben said, "Justice is delivered, let's get out of here."

He took her wrist and led her from the shop.

"Gutsy move," the envoy said.

"'Spose. I just wanted them gone."

"Drink?"

"God yes."

He pulled a small, ornate bottle of something from his pocket and put it on the counter.

She put the sword and dragon back in her pack and stowed it in a small nook concealed behind the sleeping chamber, and returned with two glasses.

He poured the alcohol and raised his glass to her.

She chinked it with her own and sipped the drink. "So, what's next?"

"Well, you need to make arrangements for 16 smuggled people."

Vee laughed, "I'd forgotten about them."

"Well, they'll be here soon, so you'd better start thinking about it."

"Hmmm," she said, rubbing her eyes with the heels of her hands. Right at that moment, it was too hard to figure out where she'd get papers and where to put them.

"But, you did a good job," the envoy said, "the Master will be pleased."

She sighed, "I never wanted to be a hero, but out on my own, I'd hoped I could help people."

"You were never going to be a hero; your skills aren't the kind heroes are made of. You're the kind of person who gets things up and running again after the heroes have trashed the place and moved on."

She snorted, "making a difference in my own way."

"I'll drink to that."

THE END

ABOUT THE AUTHOR

Alexandria Blaelock writes stories, some of them for *Ellery Queen's Mystery Magazine* and *Pulphouse Fiction Magazine*. She's also written four self-help books applying business techniques to personal matters like getting dressed, cleaning house, and feeding your friends.

As a recovering Project Manager, she's probably too fond of sticking to plan. She lives in a forest because she enjoys birdsong, the scent of gum leaves and the sun on her face. When not telecommuting to parallel universes from her Melbourne based imagination, she watches K-dramas, talks to animals, and drinks Campari. At the same time.

Discover more at www.alexandriablaelock.com.

BOOKS BY
ALEXANDRIA BLAELOCK

SHORT STORY COLLECTIONS

The Histories of Hayward Hall
Lovelorn, Lovestruck and Love at First Sight
Common or Garden Variety Heroes
Case Files of the Wilkinson Detective Agency
Unavoidable Fates
Christmas Travesties
Five Faces of Felicia Clarke

OTHER FICTION

That Love Nonsense

MS BLAELOCK'S BOOKS

Stress Free Dinner Parties
Signature Wardrobe Planning
Holistic Personal Finance
Minimally Viable Housekeeping
Planning a Life Worth Living

SELECTED SHORT STORIES

Alma's Grace
Balancing the Book
Carmelita Basingstoke
Fate in Your Hands
Kiss of Death
Lady of the Looking Glass
Life in the Security Directorate
Long Weekend in the Snow
Love in the Past Tense
Love in the Security Directorate
Morning Star, Evening Star, Superstar
Needy Bitch
Payton's Run
Phoenix Child
Secret Singer
Shining Star
Ship in a Bottle
Simone Says Hands in the Air
Special Relativity in Space
The Bygone Boyfriend
The Day the Schedule Broke
The Ghost Detectors
The Guardian's Vigil
The Mince Pie Mystery
The Mystery of the Master Suite
The Pseudonym's Bride
The Shadow Thieves
The Time-Space Paradox
Toy Soldiers